Check on Me

For Bibi, Jasper and Felix — AD
For Harvey and Ruby — JB

The ABC 'Wave' device and the 'ABC KIDS' device are
trademarks of the Australian Broadcasting Corporation and are
used under licence by HarperCollinsPublishers Australia.

First published in Australia in 2009
by HarperCollinsChildren'sBooks
a division of HarperCollinsPublishers Australia Pty Limited
ABN 36 009 913 517
harpercollins.com.au
Text copyright © Andrew Daddo 2009
Illustrations copyright © Jonathan Bentley 2009

HarperCollinsPublishers
Level 13, 201 Elizabeth Street, Sydney, NSW 2000, Australia
Unit D1, 63 Apollo Drive, Rosedale, Auckland 0632, New Zealand
A 53, Sector 57, Noida, UP, India
1 London Bridge Street, London SE1 9GF, United Kingdom
2 Bloor Street East, 20th floor, Toronto, Ontario M4W 1A8, Canada
195 Broadway, New York NY 10007, USA

National Library of Australia Cataloguing-in-Publication data:
Daddo, Andrew.
Check on me / Andrew Daddo ; illustrator, Jonathan Bentley.
1st ed
ISBN 978 0 7333 2419 2
For primary school age.
Bentley, Jonathan.
Australian Broadcasting Corporation.

A823.3

Designed and typeset by Ellie Exarchos
Colour reproduction by Graphic Print Group, Adelaide
Printed and bound in China by RR Donnelley on 128 gram Matt Art

7 6 5 4 3   15 16 17 18

Check on Me

Andrew Daddo

Jonathan Bentley

ABC
Books

My best bedtime goes exactly like this.

You take me to bed – you know the way.
Don't forget the jumps!

There has to be a story –
first from a book

and another one from your mouth.
A happily-ever-after story with
a kid like me – but it's not me –
and a dog like her, and a cat like him.

A cuddle, please.

I'll tell you the best bits of my day

and you can tell me yours.

Tuck me in with a kiss goodnight.

Oh. I'll need a drink.

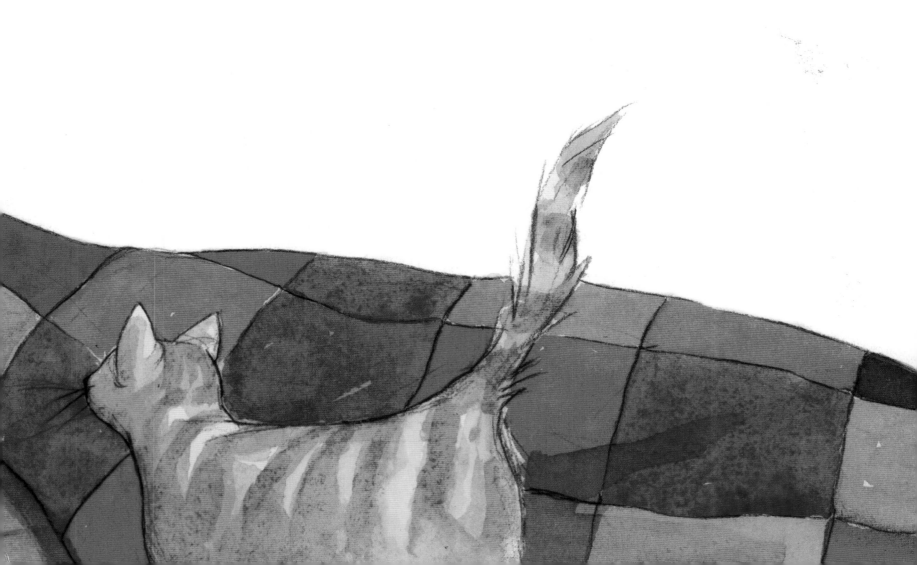

Leave the light on – just a bit –
and then I'll sleep.

But first I'd better go, just in case.

When I do sleep, it will be like

this,

and this

and this.

But that's after you fix my pillow.

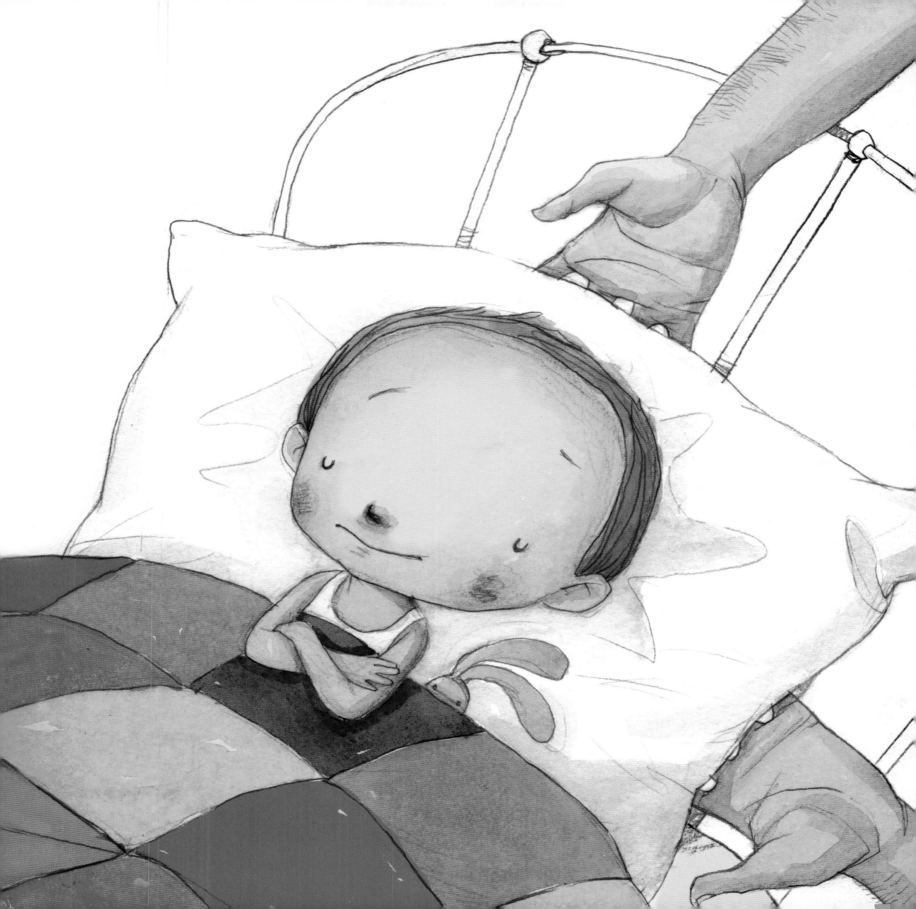

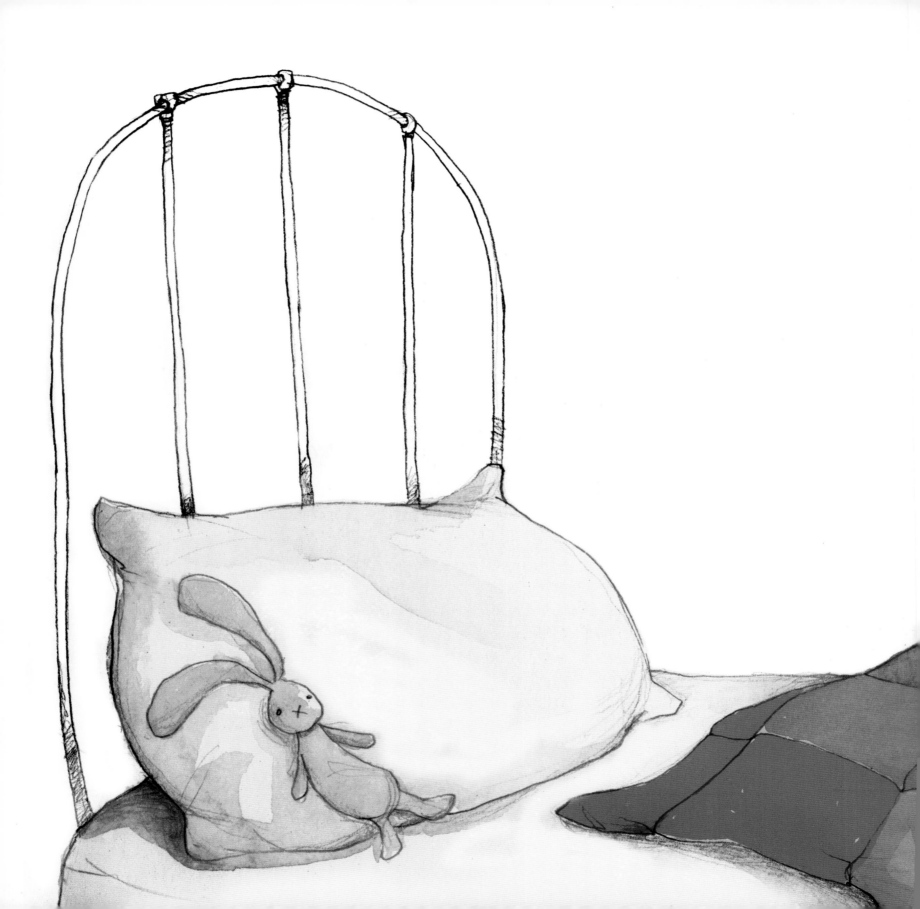

Don't forget to check on me!

You can kiss me sleeping if you like.

And if I wake up when we're all asleep,
I'll need another cuddle.

Then, in the morning I know
just the way you like to wake up!